SPACE DOG
and the
PET SHOW

Natalie Standiford

iLLUSTrated by TONy RoSS

RED FOX

A Red Fox Book

Published by Random House Children's Books
20 Vauxhall Bridge Road, London, SW1V 2SA

A division of Random House UK Ltd
London Melbourne Sydney Auckland
Johannesburg and agencies throughout the world

1 3 5 7 9 10 8 6 4 2

First published by Avon Books Ltd, New York 1990
First published in Great Britain by Hutchinson Children's Books 1991
Red Fox edition 1992
Reprinted 1993

This Red Fox edition 1999

Printed and bound in Great Britain by
Cox & Wyman Limited, Reading, Berkshire

Papers used by Random House UK Limited are natural, recyclable products
made from wood grown in sustainable forests. The manufacturing processes
conform to the environmental regulations of the country of origin.

RANDOM HOUSE UK Limited Reg. No. 954009

ISBN 0 09 940213 0

Contents

Chapter 1

Time for a Walk

'Roy,' said Mr Barnes one sunny after-noon, 'don't you ever take that dog of yours for a walk? He looks as if he could do with some exercise.'

Roy Barnes and his dog, Space Dog, were watching tennis on TV. It was a lazy Saturday in summer. Roy's father had come into the living room to find out what the score was.

'Space Dog runs in the back garden,' Roy said to his father.

Mr Barnes looked at Space Dog's stom-ach. 'It doesn't look like it,' he said. 'He's getting podgy.'

Space Dog shifted uncomfortably. He didn't like it when Mr Barnes talked about him as if he wasn't there.

'Come on, Roy,' said Mr Barnes. 'It's a nice day. Get off your backside and take the dog for a walk.'

'OK,' said Roy. Mr Barnes left the room. 'Want to go for a walk, Space Dog?' Roy asked.

'You know I don't,' said Space Dog. 'I hate walks. I hate leads. I hate being seen walking on all fours. I hate the whole thing.'

'Come on,' said Roy, standing up. 'Dad will get cross if we don't go. Besides, you *are* getting podgy.'

'Thanks a lot,' said Space Dog.

Space Dog wasn't used to going for walks. He wasn't used to doing anything like a normal dog. Space Dog was a creature from outer space who just hap-

pened to look exactly like a dog. He was a
citizen of the planet Queekrg, and he was
used to talking and reading and walking
on two legs like Earth people.

His spaceship had crash-landed in Roy's back garden and ever since, he had forced himself to behave like an Earth dog to keep his alien identity a secret. His mission for his home planet was to gather new information about Earth. Only Roy knew who Space Dog really was.

Roy went and got Space Dog's lead and the two of them set off. Space Dog dragged his feet unhappily as they walked down the street.

'Come on,' said Roy. 'Most dogs love going for walks. They wag their tails and sniff around . . .'

'And closely examine lamp posts!' said Space Dog. 'It's disgusting.'

Space Dog and Roy walked to a small grocery shop. Roy bought two choc ices, one for each of them. Then they went outside and sat on the curb. Roy unwrapped the ices and held one out to Space Dog. Space Dog reached for it.

'Don't!' said Roy, pulling his hand back. 'I have to hold the ice cream for you. You don't want anyone to see you holding it.'

'But I hate it when you feed me,' said Space Dog. 'It makes me feel like an idiot.'

'Do you want me to put the ice cream on the ground?' said Roy. 'That's the only other way an Earth dog would eat it.'

'Don't you dare!' said Space Dog. 'I will not eat a choc ice covered with dirt!'

'Well?' said Roy. 'What should I do?'

Space Dog looked at the choc ice. It was beginning to melt. His mouth watered. 'All right' he said. 'Quick! Feed me before it melts.'

Space Dog and Roy slurped down their ice creams. When they had finished, Roy stood up. A sign on a lamp post caught his eye. The sign said:

CHILDREN'S PET SHOW SATURDAY JONES St. PARK ALL PETS WELCOME ROSETTES FOR THE WINNERS!

'Look at this!' said Roy.

Space Dog read the sign. 'So?' he said.

'I've always wanted to enter a pet show—but I've never had a pet before! Let's do it. You'll win a prize for certain!'

'Wait a minute, Roy,' said Space Dog. 'You want to enter *me* in a pet show? What do you think I am, a pet?'

'Well, no,' said Roy. 'But it would be fun! There's probably a prize for the cleverest dog. You could win that one hands down!'

'I don't need any pet-show judge to tell me I'm clever,' said Space Dog.

But Roy was hardly listening. 'I've never won anything in my whole life,' he said. 'If we win first place, we'll get a blue rosette!'

'No, no and no!' said Space Dog. 'I will not compete with a bunch of drooling, howling, scratching animals! And that's final.'

Roy sighed. 'OK,' he said. 'I suppose I'll

have to try and win a rosette some other way.' He turned and started home.

'I'm sorry, Roy,' said Space Dog, trotting by Roy's side. 'But don't you think a dog show is rather stupid? You'd be much better off winning something important, like a spelling competition.'

'Yes,' said Roy. 'A pet show. Big deal.'

Chapter 2

Space Dog Changes his Mind

When Space Dog and Roy were nearly home, they saw Alice and Blanche waiting for them on the front steps. Alice lived next door. She and Roy were friends. Blanche was Alice's poodle. When Blanche saw Space Dog, she ran up to him.

'Oh, no,' Space Dog whispered to Roy. 'Here comes birdbrain Blanche. Protect me, Roy!'

Blanche adored Space Dog. But Space Dog couldn't stand Blanche. For one thing, she wanted to kiss him.

Blanche tried to rub noses with Space Dog. He backed away and hid behind Roy.

'Hi, Roy,' said Alice, getting up off the steps. Alice was as messy-looking as always. Her socks were falling down, and her plaits were coming undone.

'Hi, Alice,' said Roy. 'Would you mind holding on to Blanche? She gets on Space Dog's nerves.'

Alice called Blanche. Then she knelt down and patted her poodle. 'I don't understand it,' said Alice. 'Blanche is so

sweet and so pretty. Why doesn't Space Dog like her?'

So sweet? So pretty? Space Dog rolled his eyes.

Roy said, 'She's always trying to kiss him. I think that's why he doesn't like her.'

'Most dogs like to be kissed,' said Alice. She kissed Blanche on top of her head. 'See? Blanche loves it.'

'Well, Space Dog isn't Blanche,' said Roy.

'Blanche is going to win at the pet show,' said Alice. 'Did you hear about it? I think a pet show is exciting.'

Roy glanced at Space Dog. Space Dog yawned.

'Yes, I heard about it,' said Roy. 'But I'm not going to enter Space Dog.'

'Why not?' asked Alice.

'It'll be boring,' said Roy.

'Boring?' said Alice. 'I bet you're afraid Space Dog wouldn't win a prize. He *is* rather funny-looking.'

'He is not!' said Roy.

'And he can't even fetch a ball,' said Alice.

'That's not true!' said Roy. 'Sometimes he's just not in the mood. That's all.'

'Well, Blanche is sure to win something,' said Alice. 'She's the prettiest, cleverest, best all-round dog in the world!'

Space Dog looked at Blanche. Then he looked at Roy.

'Down, boy,' said Roy.

'Well,' said Alice, 'Blanche and I are going home to practise some tricks. The pet show is only a week away!' She stood up. 'Come on, Blanche.'

'Bye, Alice,' said Roy. 'Bye, Blanche.'

When they had gone, Space Dog said, 'Did you hear that? Alice called that walking vegetable of hers clever!'

'Yes,' said Roy. 'And she called *you* funny-looking.'

'I know,' said Space Dog. 'But what I really can't believe is how anyone could think that curly-haired dodo is brighter than I am! I'll show them. I *will* enter that pet show!'

'You will?' said Roy. 'Do you promise? Cross your heart and hope to die?'

'Yes,' said Space Dog. 'I promise.'

'That's great!' said Roy. 'But why did you change your mind?'

'Dignity, Roy,' said Space Dog. 'I've got to enter that show to uphold my personal dignity.'

Chapter 3

A Game of Fish

Roy was really happy. Space Dog was actually going to do something doggy for a change. Then everybody would see what a great dog he had. And he would win a rosette. Roy could hardly wait.

On Sunday Roy thought more about the pet show. He and Space Dog needed to have a talk about Space Dog's training.

Space Dog was up in Roy's room, reading a sports magazine and eating popcorn. He loved popcorn. What he didn't like was dog food.

'Well now, Space Dog,' said Roy. 'We have less than a week to get ready for the

pet show. We've got to get you into shape.'
He snatched the bag of popcorn away
from Space Dog. 'No more popcorn! From
now on you're on a diet. Fruit and
vegetables.'

'What?' said Space Dog. 'Who said so?'

'I do,' said Roy. 'And make sure you jog
around the back garden for twenty
minutes each day.'

'What has that got to do with the pet
show?' asked Space Dog. 'I'm going to
show them how clever I am, not how big
my muscles are. Huh!'

'You never know what the judges will be
looking for,' said Roy. 'If they are busy
staring at your pot belly, they won't notice
how clever you are.'

'They'll notice, all right,' said Space Dog.
'I'll write out any maths problem they
want. I'll recite poetry in ancient Greek. I'll
tell them my theory about why dinosaurs

are extinct. How can I lose?'

'Space Dog!' said Roy in alarm. 'You can't do things like that at the pet show! Everyone will know you're an alien!'

'Just kidding,' said Space Dog.

'Oh,' said Roy. 'Well, talking Greek isn't a good trick for a pet show anyway.'

'What *is* a good trick?' asked Space Dog.

'You have to do things that Earth dogs do. Sit. Roll over. Heel.'

'I'm no good at those things!' said Space Dog.

'You can learn,' said Roy. 'You can go into training, starting today.'

'But can I roll over and still keep my dignity?' said Space Dog. 'That is the question.'

'Just think of Blanche with a blue rosette on her collar,' said Roy.

'OK, OK,' said Space Dog. 'Just tell me what to do.'

Just then the doorbell rang. A minute later Roy heard his mother calling. 'Roy! Alice is here!'

'You go and talk to Alice,' said Space Dog. 'I want to read some more about golf.' He opened the magazine again.

Roy went downstairs. Alice was waiting for him. Her shirt was half in and half out. One trainer was untied.

'Hi, Roy,' she said.

'Hi,' said Roy. 'Want to play cards?'

'OK.'

Alice sat on the living-room rug. Roy got a pack of cards from a drawer in the kitchen. Then he sat on the rug opposite Alice.

Roy dealt the cards and they began to play.

'Got any twos?' asked Alice.

'Fish,' said Roy.

They played the game for a while and didn't talk except when they asked each other for cards.

At last Alice said, 'I'm so excited about the pet show. Are you going to come and cheer for Blanche?'

'I'll be there,' said Roy. 'But I'm going to cheer for Space Dog. Got any jacks?'

'Fish,' said Alice. 'I thought you said pet shows were boring.'

'Not with Space Dog around,' said Roy.

'Besides, he's going to win.'

'He is not,' said Alice. 'He's too funny-looking. Got any tens?'

'Fish,' said Roy. 'Who cares what he looks like? He's clever. Really clever. You can't even imagine how clever.'

'He can't fetch,' said Alice 'He can't do any tricks.'

'He'll know plenty of tricks by next Saturday,' said Roy. 'Got any aces?'

'Fish,' said Alice. 'I still think he's too funny-looking to win. Look at Blanche. She's beautiful. But I'm still not taking any chances. On Friday, I'm going to take her to Dottie's Dog Salon. After that, she'll be knockout. Got any jacks?'

'Rats,' said Roy. He gave the jack in his hand to Alice. 'What's Dottie's Dog Salon?'

'It's in Bede Street,' said Alice. 'It's a beauty parlour for dogs. Got any aces?'

Roy handed her an ace and said, 'What do they do there?'

'They wash dogs and clip their coats. They can even paint their toenails if you want. That's what I'm going to tell them to do to Blanche. Won't she look great with red toenails?'

Roy scowled. 'That's the stupidest thing I've ever heard.'

'It is not,' said Alice. 'When the judges at the pet show see Blanche, they'll go nuts. Got any fives?'

'A beauty parlour for dogs?' said Roy slowly. 'Maybe they could make Space Dog look better. Maybe it's not so stupid. Can I bring Space Dog and go with you on Friday?'

'Of course,' said Alice. 'It's OK with me. No matter what they do to Space Dog, he'll never be as pretty as Blanche. Got any fives?' she asked again.

Roy handed Alice a five. Then she put down her cards and said, 'I won!'

Chapter 4

It's Training Time

Roy put off telling Space Dog about the beauty parlour. Something told him Space Dog wasn't going to like the idea.

Maybe he would tell Space Dog later in the week. Maybe he would tell him on the way to Dottie's. Roy knew it wasn't right to keep Space Dog in the dark, but he wanted to win a rosette at the pet show more than anything.

Before he got out of bed on Monday morning, Roy decided it was time to get to work. Even if Dottie's Dog Salon made Space Dog look fantastic, he still needed to learn some tricks.

As soon as Space Dog was awake, Roy said, 'I know what we can do today.'

'So do I,' said Space Dog. 'We can bake some biscuits. We can make double-chocolate chips!'

'Or,' said Roy, 'we can practise a few tricks for the pet show.'

'*Or* we can make biscuits,' said Space Dog.

'We can do both,' said Roy.

'But think how many biscuits we could make if we did nothing but bake all day!' said Space Dog.

'Oh no!' said Roy. 'First we practise tricks. *Then* we can bake some biscuits.'

'I suppose there is no way out,' said Space Dog. 'But I won't do any tricks before breakfast.'

Roy went down to the kitchen by himself. He ate a bowl of cereal. By the time he'd finished, his mother was out of the kitchen. Then he filled a bowl of cereal for Space Dog and took it up to his room.

'I hope it's not mushy,' he said. 'I had to put the milk in downstairs.'

Roy had got used to feeding Space Dog in his room. That way, Space Dog could eat human food without Mr and Mrs Barnes knowing. He was supposed to eat dog food, but dog food made him sick.

'Thanks,' said Space Dog. 'It's fine.'

When Space Dog had eaten his cereal,
Roy said, 'It's training time.'

Roy picked up the empty bowl. Space
Dog followed him downstairs. Roy went
into the kitchen and put the bowl in the
dishwasher so his mother wouldn't see it.
Then the two friends went out to the back
garden.

'What kind of tricks do you want to do?'
asked Roy.

'I don't want to do *any* tricks,' said Space Dog. 'How many times do I have to tell you?'

Roy went on. 'How about this one?' he said. He got down on his hands and knees.

'When I say, "Beg", this is what you do,' said Roy. He sat back on his heels. He held his hands out in front of him like paws. Then Roy let his tongue hang out while he panted.

'I don't like that one,' said Space Dog.

'OK,' said Roy. 'How about this? I hold up a hoop, and you jump through it.'

'Not my style,' said Space Dog. 'Not at *all*.'

'Never mind,' said Roy. 'I have another idea. I'll ask you a maths question, and you give me the answer.'

'That's not bad,' said Space Dog.

'Let's try it,' said Roy. 'We'll pretend we're at the show.' He cleared his throat and said loudly, 'Space Dog, what is one and one?'

'Two,' said Space Dog.

'No, no!' said Roy. 'You don't *say* the answer. You stamp it out with your foot. Ready?'

'Ready.'

'Space Dog, how much is one and two?'

Space Dog stamped his foot on the ground three times.

'That's great!' said Roy. 'That will really knock their socks off!'

'I have another idea,' said Space Dog. 'First, you ask me easy questions, like one and one. The judges will think that's all we can do, but then we will surprise them.'

'Will we?' said Roy.

'Of course,' said Space Dog. 'After the easy questions, you ask me a hard question. Then everyone will be really amazed when I get the answer right. What do you think?'

'Sounds like a good idea,' said Roy.

Space Dog smiled. 'This is great!' he said. 'And I don't mind doing this trick. This is one silly old Blanche could never do. I bet she can't even count to ten.'

'I'm sure she can't,' said Roy. 'Most dogs don't do much counting.'

'Well,' said Space Dog. 'I think that's enough training for one day, don't you?'

'What about the other tricks?' said Roy.

'This trick is so good,' said Space Dog, 'we don't need any others.'

'But—'

'Now, Roy, listen to your old friend. We've got that pet show all sewn up. Stop worrying, OK?'

'OK,' said Roy.

'Now, on to the biscuits!' said Space Dog. 'I saw a recipe in the Sunday paper. Your mother bought some chocolate chips last week—which are just what we need. Oh, I love Earth food!'

Space Dog led the way into the house— and made a beeline for the kitchen!

Chapter 5

Dottie's Dog Salon

For the next few days, Roy and Space Dog didn't talk much about the pet show. Once a day or so Roy would get nervous and say, 'Shouldn't we practise our trick, Space Dog?'

Space Dog would smile and tell Roy not to worry. 'It's in the bag, Roy! Believe me!'

Roy tried to stop worrying, but he was afraid Space Dog was being lazy. He thought *that* was the reason Space Dog wouldn't practise the trick.

The truth was that Space Dog was sure they had everything worked out. He was sure the adding trick would be easy, so

easy that there was no need to practise. Instead, he ate popcorn and did his research for the rest of the week. Little did he know what Roy had in store for him on Friday.

When Friday morning came, only Roy knew that he and Space Dog were going to go to Dottie's Dog Salon. But first Roy needed some money to pay for it.

That morning Roy went to his parents' bedroom. His mother was working at her desk.

'Hey, Mum,' said Roy. 'Remember the pet show I told you about?'

'Yes,' said Mrs Barnes. She looked up from her work.

'Remember I said I was going to enter Space Dog?' said Roy.

'Yes, dear, I do,' said Mrs Barnes. 'Maybe Space Dog will win a special prize. He *is* unusual.'

'I hope so,' said Roy. 'But Alice says he's funny-looking.'

'Oh?' Mrs Barnes wasn't paying attention any more. She looked back at her desk.

'Space Dog might look better,' said Roy, 'if he was tidied up a little bit.'

'He might,' said Mrs Barnes, half listening. 'Or he might not.'

'I know a place that can do it,' Roy went on. 'Dottie's Dog Salon.'

Mrs Barnes looked up from her desk. 'Dottie's Dog Salon?' she said. 'Where they paint dog's toenails? And dye their hair?'

'That's right,' said Roy. 'Don't you think they could help?'

'I think Space Dog could end up looking funnier than ever,' said Mrs Barnes. 'But give it a try. How much does it cost?'

'Alice says it's five pounds,' said Roy. 'That's for a bath and a clip.'

Mrs Barnes reached for her purse. She gave Roy a five-pound note. 'Go ahead,' she told him. 'I'd like to see Space Dog afterwards.'

'Thanks, Mum!' said Roy.

Roy went into the kitchen for Space Dog's lead. Then he went outside to the kennel. Space Dog was there, busy reading.

'Hi, Space Dog,' said Roy.

'Hi, Roy,' said Space Dog. 'I'm just finishing my golf report. No one from my planet has ever reported on golf before.'

'That's great,' said Roy. 'How would you like to go for a walk?' Roy still didn't have the courage to tell Space Dog about Dottie's.

'Again?' said Space Dog. 'I had a walk last Saturday.'

'Come on,' said Roy feeling miserable. 'It's good for you.' Roy snapped the lead on to Space Dog's collar and off they went.

Soon Space Dog noticed that Roy was taking him a different route from usual. 'Where are we going?' asked Space Dog.

'To Bede Street,' Roy said.

'Why?' asked Space Dog.

'Oh, just for a change,' said Roy, trying to pretend nothing was going on.

They walked a bit farther. Then they turned into a busy street, with lots of shops and restaurants in it.

'Well, we're in Bede Street,' said Space Dog. 'Can we turn round now?'

'I—uh—want to stop somewhere first,' said Roy.

'Something's up,' said Space Dog. 'I can

feel it. Roy, where are we going?'

Roy stopped in front of a shop. The glass in the shop window was pink. The big sign over the shop window was pink. It said, DOTTIE'S DOG SALON.

People were walking past them on the pavement. 'Here we are,' Roy said quietly. He didn't want anyone to hear him talking to Space Dog.

Space Dog looked up. He saw the sign. 'Oh, no!' he said. 'I'm not going in there!'

'Shh!' said Roy. Then he whispered, 'I'm sorry I didn't tell you about it earlier but if you want to win a prize at the pet show, you have to look nice.'

'But I *do* look nice!' whispered Space Dog. 'I'm the nicest-looking fellow I know!'

'Blanche is being done here,' whispered Roy. 'So you have to, too.'

Roy pulled Space Dog's lead. There was a tug-of-war. In the end, Roy dragged Space Dog into Dottie's.

Alice and Blanche were already there. They sat at the front, waiting their turn.

'Hi, Roy!' said Alice. 'I thought maybe you weren't coming.'

Roy pulled Space Dog towards a chair. 'I thought maybe we weren't coming, too,' said Roy. 'Space Dog doesn't like it here.'

Alice patted Blanche on the head. 'Blanche can't wait,' said Alice. 'She loves Dottie's. She has a real poodle personality.'

A woman came out from behind a pink curtain. She had curly blonde hair. She wore a pink smock that said *Dottie* on it.

'Alice?' said the woman. 'Is Blanche ready?'

'She certainly is,' said Alice. She and Blanche got up and walked to the back.

'And who are you?' Dottie asked Roy.

'My name is Roy, and this is Space Dog,' said Roy. 'Would you give him a bath?'

'Space Dog!' said Dottie. 'Now I've heard everything. Well, it's nice to meet you. Why don't you two come on through with Alice and Blanche? My assistant, Belle, can work on Space Dog while I bath Blanche.'

'Great,' said Roy. He started towards the room in the rear.

Space Dog didn't follow. 'Come *on*,' said Roy. 'You might as well get it over with.'

'I'm going to hate this,' muttered Space Dog. He trudged off after Roy.

In the back room were two big baths and two padded tables. A red-haired woman stood by one of the baths. Her pink smock said BELLE on it.

Belle knelt by Space Dog and patted him. 'Who is this cutesy-wootsy little fellow?' she asked.

'His name is Space Dog,' said Roy.

'He's adora-worable,' said Belle. Then she patted the side of the bath. 'Come on, cutesy,' she said. 'Get in.'

Space Dog sighed and allowed himself to be put into the bath. Belle washed him while Dottie washed Blanche. Roy and Alice sat nearby and watched.

Belle took a bottle and poured some brown liquid into her hand. The stuff smelled horrible.

'This will kill your fleas,' Belle told Space Dog. 'We don't want any buggies in your fur, do we?'

I don't have fleas, madam, Space Dog said to himself.

'He doesn't have fleas,' Roy said to Belle. 'You don't have to put that stuff on him.'

'Too late,' said Belle, rubbing in the flea shampoo.

'So, cutesy,' she said, squirting Space Dog with a hose, 'what about that pretty little poodle you came in with? Is she your girlfriend?' Belle pointed to Blanche.

Space Dog looked at Blanche. She was having her fur fluffed after her bath. Blanche looked back at him sweetly.

I don't have a girlfriend, madam, Space Dog said silently.

'He doesn't have a girlfriend,' said Roy. He wished Belle wouldn't talk about Blanche.

Belle lifted Space Dog out of the bath and on to the padded table. She began to put curlers in his fur. 'If there's one thing

I like,' she said, 'It's a curly-haired dog. I'm going to make you look just as nice as your girlfriend Blanche. My, she is a pretty little poodle. You've got good taste in girl-friends, sweetie-pie.'

Space Dog could hardly stand any more of this. Blanche stood still happily while Dottie clipped her coat. She seemed to understand every word Belle said. She looked at Space Dog and drooled with love.

'So what do you and Blanchie-poo do on your dates?' Belle was saying. 'Do you have nice doggie dinners?'

I'm going to be sick! thought Space Dog.

'Really, Blanche is *not* his girlfriend,' said Roy. 'And I don't think you should tease him so much.'

Belle stopped working and put her hands on her hips. 'Well, for heaven's sake,' she said. 'Your dog doesn't know I'm teasing him. He's just a dog after all!'

'He *does* know you're teasing!' said Roy, before he could stop himself. 'Well, I mean animals are clever. Some of them are really clever.'

Space Dog smiled to himself. *Thanks, Roy,* he said silently.

Dottie had finished trimming Blanche's coat. Now she was painting Blanche's toenails red.

Belle blow-dried Space Dog and took

out his curlers. 'If you like his curls,' she
told Roy, 'I could give him a permanent
wave next time you come.'

Then she tied pink ribbons through
Space Dog's new curls. 'We could put a
nice blue rinse in his coat next time,' Belle
said. 'It would cover up the grey.'

'No, thanks,' said Roy. 'He likes the grey.
It makes him look mature.'

'Oh? Maybe you're right,' said Belle.

At last both dogs were done. Blanche had an old-fashioned poodle cut. She looked like a puffy set of balls. Also, her toenails were fire-engine red. She looked very fancy—and very proud.

'Blanchie!' said Alice, giving her a hug. 'You look like a beauty queen!'

Space Dog looked at Blanche. He thought she looked more ridiculous than ever.

Roy looked at Space Dog. He was all curls and little pink ribbons. Roy didn't say a word.

'Doesn't he look fabu-wabulous?' said Belle. 'That will be five pounds, please.'

Roy paid Belle, and Alice paid Dottie. Then they put the leads on the dogs and left the salon.

'Blanche can't lose now,' said Alice as they all walked down the street together. 'Look at those toenails! Wow!'

'Space Dog looks nice, too, I think,' said Roy. But he wasn't at all sure.

When they were close to home, Alice began to jog a little faster. 'I can't wait until my mother sees Blanche!' she said. 'See you later, Roy!' And she ran towards her house with Blanche close behind.

Roy and Space Dog had almost reached home. Since Alice had gone, Space Dog could talk at last. 'Roy!' he exploded. 'How could you do this to me? I look awful!'

'I think you look adora-worable,' Roy joked.

'It's not funny!' said Space Dog. 'I agreed to enter the pet show for the sake of my dignity. But this—this—' He pointed to a pink ribbon. This is humiliation!'

'Calm down,' said Roy. 'We can take the ribbons out as soon as we get home. But the curly hair isn't so bad. Let's see what mum says.'

Chapter 6

Getting Ready

When Roy and Space Dog got home, Mrs Barnes was waiting for them. She looked at Space Dog and put her hand over her mouth.

'Oh, *goodness*, Roy,' she said. 'Doesn't he look—' Mrs Barnes had to stop. Behind her hand, she was trying not to laugh. Quickly she left the room.

'That does it,' said Space Dog. 'I must take these ribbons out of my hair AT ONCE!'

They went upstairs to Roy's room. Roy helped untie the ribbons. 'I'm sorry, Space Dog,' he said. 'I thought the beauty parlour was a good idea, but I was wrong. Still, it was sort of fun.'

'Fun for you maybe,' said Space Dog. 'But no one is laughing at you!'

'I know,' said Roy. He pulled out the last of the ribbons.

'I should just get out of this pet show once and for all,' said Space Dog. 'From now on I should spend all my time in the basement, repairing my spaceship, and then fly back to Queekrg as soon as possible!'

'Don't say that!' said Roy. 'Look, all the ribbons are out. You don't have to look fancy for the pet show. You can just be clever. Your trick will be great!'

'I don't want to do my trick. I do not want to go.'

Suddenly Roy sounded very serious. 'Space Dog, you promised,' he said.

'I don't remember that,' said Space Dog.

'You *did*,' said Roy. 'You can't back out now. And what if Blanche wins a prize? Alice will never shut up about it. My life

won't be worth living.'

Space Dog thought. Roy was right. Curls or no curls, he had to keep his promise. He had to enter the pet show.

At last it was Saturday. Roy had set the alarm so he and Space Dog would get up in plenty of time for the show. When the alarm went off, Roy got out of bed at once. 'Today is the big day, Space Dog,' he said.

Space Dog opened his eyes. 'The big day?' he said with a yawn.

'The pet show, silly,' said Roy. 'Get up and start getting ready. I'll go downstairs and try to get you a hot breakfast. I want you to have lots of energy today.'

Roy went downstairs. His mother was frying two eggs for him. 'Good morning, Mum,' he said.

'Good morning, Roy,' said Mrs Barnes. She put the plate of eggs down on the

table. Roy got himself a glass of orange juice.

'Are you nervous about the pet show today?' asked Mrs Barnes.

'A little bit,' Roy admitted. 'But I shouldn't worry. It's in the bag.'

'How do you know?' asked Mrs Barnes.

Roy almost said, 'Because Space Dog says so.' But he stopped himself. 'I just know,' he said.

'Well, good luck,' said Mrs Barnes. 'I'll be thinking of you.'

'Thanks, Mum,' said Roy. 'Could I have

some more eggs, please?' He held out his plate.

'More!' said Mrs Barnes. 'You certainly have been eating a lot lately.'

'I think my stomach is growing,' said Roy.

Mrs Barnes fried two more eggs. Then, while she wasn't looking, Roy slipped the eggs into a napkin. He took them upstairs as soon as he could, with a glass of orange juice.

Space Dog was in Roy's room, drying off. He had just had a shower. His fur looked straighter than the day before, but there was still some curl left in it.

Roy opened his desk drawer and took out a paper plate. Then he found some salt and a plastic knife and fork.

'Here's your breakfast,' Roy said. Then he sniffed the air. 'What is that smell?' he asked.

'Aftershave,' said Space Dog. 'I found it in your parents' bathroom. Do you like it?'

'It's awful,' said Roy. 'Why did you put it on?'

'To smell nice for the pet show,' said Space Dog. 'Should I wash it off?'

'No,' said Roy. 'We don't have time. Eat your breakfast.'

Space Dog ate his breakfast while Roy got dressed. Soon they were ready to go. For the first time, Space Dog didn't complain when Roy snapped the lead on to his collar. For that one day, Space Dog was willing to act like a dog.

'Ready?' asked Roy.

'Ready as I'll ever be,' said Space Dog.

And off they went.

Chapter 7

The Pet Show

The pet show was held in the Jones Street Park. The day was sunny. A cool breeze blew through the trees. The park was swarming with children and pets. Most of the pets were dogs and cats.

The children with dogs were supposed to go to an open space in the middle of the park. That's where Roy and Space Dog went.

On a table in the centre of the dog area were rows and rows of rosettes, blue, red and white. Roy walked up to look at them. He knew the white ones were for third place. The red ones were for second. The blue rosettes were for first. The rosettes were for MOST OBEDIENT, BIGGEST, SMALLEST, CALMEST, WAGGIEST TAIL, PRETTIEST, and CUTEST.

Then Space Dog saw one more, the one he had been looking for—MOST INTELLIGENT. He nudged Roy. 'That's the one we're going to win,' he whispered.

'I hope so,' Roy said quietly. 'But I'd be glad to have any of these. Could you win MOST OBEDIENT?'

Space Dog shook his head. 'Are you joking?' he whispered.

The children and their dogs were gathering round in a big circle. Roy saw lots of different kinds of dogs. There were tiny lap dogs and huge Great Danes. There were shaggy dogs and neat dogs, skinny dogs and roly-poly dogs. Some of them barked and others whined.

Roy saw Alice and Blanche. He and Space Dog went over to stand next to

them. Alice had tied a red bow round
Blanche's neck. The colour went with her
toenails. There were red bows round Alice's plaits, too. But of course they had
come undone.

'Hi, Roy,' said Alice. 'Are you ready?'

'I think so,' said Roy. 'Space Dog has
learned a good trick.'

'Blanche knows a good one, too,' said
Alice. Then she sniffed. 'What's that funny
smell?'

'Aftershave,' said Roy.

'Oh,' said Alice.

A woman in a red cap stood up and clapped her hands. 'Quiet, everyone,' she shouted. The dogs and their owners quietened down. 'My name is Manya,' said the woman. 'And this is Fred.'

She pointed to a man in a blue T-shirt and glasses. He held a clipboard and pencil. 'We will be the judges today. Is everyone ready?'

'Yes,' said the children.

'Woof,' said the dogs.

'Then let's begin. We will go round the circle and look at each dog. When we get to you, show us the trick your dog can do. After we have looked at all the dogs, we will announce the winners.'

Fred and Manya started on the far side of the circle from Roy and Alice. The first dog they looked at was a Great Dane called Harold. Harold stood up while Fred and Manya examined him. Then Harold's owner, a little girl called Muffy, said, 'Sit!' Harold sat, and Muffy patted him.

'Thank you, Muffy,' said Fred. He made a note on his clipboard.

'I think Harold will win Biggest Dog,' Alice whispered to Roy. 'Don't you?'

Roy looked around. He couldn't see any dogs bigger than Harold. 'I expect so,' he said.

Next was a Irish red setter called Joyce. Joyce's owner was a freckle-faced boy called Boyce.

Boyce took a harmonica from his pocket. He put it to his mouth and began to play *Oranges and Lemons*. Joyce sat up and howled while Boyce played. 'Aaaoow! Aaaoow!' Some of the children blocked their ears.

When the howling was over, Manya

said, 'That was lovely, Boyce.' Fred made
another note on his clipboard, and they
moved on to the next dog.

'Joyce doesn't have a chance,' whispered Alice.

'I just wish they would hurry up,' said
Roy. 'This makes me nervous.'

Space Dog didn't mind waiting while
the judges went from dog to dog. To him,
none of the dogs seemed very bright.

Space Dog was sure he was going to win MOST INTELLIGENT.

At last Fred and Manya came round to Alice. 'And who are you?' asked Manya.

'My name is Alice,' said Alice. 'And this is my dog, Blanche. She has red nail polish on her toenails.'

They looked at Blanche's toenails. 'Very nice,' said Fred.

'Blanche knows a lot of tricks,' said Alice. 'I've chosen the best one. Watch this.' Alice turned to Blanche and said, 'Somersault, Blanche! Somersault!'

Blanche was standing up. First she tucked her head down. Then she did a perfect forward somersault.

'Good girl!' said Alice.

'That was very impressive,' said Manya. 'Thank you, Alice.'

While Fred wrote on his pad, Roy whispered in Alice's ear. 'That was pretty good!' he said.

'I know,' said Alice.

Space Dog made a face. *That was pretty sickening*, he said to himself.

But now it was Space Dog's turn. Roy

cleared his throat and said, 'My name is Roy and this is Space Dog. Space Dog can count.'

Someone in the crowd shouted, '*Sure* he can!' Everybody laughed.

'Quiet, everyone,' said Manya.

'He really *can* count,' said Roy. 'Watch.' He turned to Space Dog. 'Space Dog, what is two and two?'

Easy, thought Space Dog. He stamped four times with his front paw. Roy bowed and said, 'Ta da!'

'Thank you, Roy,' said Manya. She and Fred began to turn to the next dog.

'Wait!' said Roy quickly. 'There's more.'

Fred and Manya watched again. Roy said, 'Space Dog, what is five minus one?'

Another easy one, thought Space Dog. He stamped the ground four times. And once again, Roy said 'Ta da!'

'Four is the only number he knows!'

somebody in the crowd called out.

'It is not!' Roy shouted.

'That's all right, Roy,' said Manya. 'I like your dog's little curls. Now we have to move on.'

But Roy couldn't stop. 'You haven't seen the best part,' he said. 'Space Dog's just done the easy ones. Now he will answer a hard question.'

Gosh, he sounds nervous, thought Space Dog.

'Space Dog,' said Roy, 'what is three hundred and fifty-six times two hundred and seventy-five?'

Space Dog thought for a second. Then he began to stamp the ground. He stamped and stamped and stamped and stamped.

The crowd got tired of watching Space Dog.

'He doesn't know the answer,' one boy shouted. 'He's just stamping his paw!'

'He *does* know the answer!' said Roy.

'I'm sure he does,' said Manya. 'But we're

running out of time, Roy. We'll have to move on.'

Fred made a mark on his clipboard. He and Manya moved to the next dog.

Space Dog was still stamping away. Roy knelt beside him and said quietly, 'You can stop now.'

'But I haven't stamped out the answer yet,' whispered Space Dog.

'What *is* the answer?' whispered Roy.

'Ninety-seven thousand, nine hundred,' said Space Dog. He stopped stamping.

'I think we messed it up,' Roy said sadly.

'I don't see why,' said Space Dog. 'I'm clearly the most intelligent dog within miles of this park.'

'Yes, but the judges still don't know that,' said Roy.

'Don't you think we'll win a prize?' asked Space Dog.

Roy shook his head.

'Then let's leave,' said Space Dog.

Roy stood up. He turned to say goodbye to Alice. 'We're going home,' he said.

'Why?' asked Alice. 'Don't you want to see Blanche win her prize? And Space Dog might win, too.'

'I don't think so,' said Roy.

'Space Dog's trick was great,' said Alice. 'Maybe you'll win something. Anyway, the show is almost over.'

'OK,' said Roy. 'We'll stay.'

When the judges had looked at the very last dog, they stood by the table and had a meeting. The children sat and waited with their dogs.

Finally Manya and Fred turned round. 'It's time to announce the winners,' Manya said, in a loud voice. 'You all have wonderful dogs. We've had a difficult time choosing. But anyway, here goes. Third place for

Biggest Dog goes to Jenny and her dog, Jumbo!'

Everyone clapped. Jenny and Jumbo, a big, wide German shepherd, ran up to Manya and Fred. Fred gave Jenny a white rosette and shook her hand.

Then Manya and Fred gave out most of the other awards. None of them went to Roy and Space Dog. But none of them went to Blanche, either. And there were still two rosettes left. One was the blue rosette for MOST INTELLIGENT. Roy didn't think Space Dog had a chance, but he crossed his fingers anyway.

'First place for Most Intelligent Dog,' said Manya, 'goes to Alice and her dog, Blanche!'

'Hurray!' shouted Alice. The other children clapped. Alice ran up to Fred for the rosette. Roy and Space Dog just looked at each other, as if to say, *I can't believe it!'*

Alice came back and pinned the rosette to Blanche's red ribbon. Blanche's tongue was hanging out. She was panting with pride.

'Congratulations,' said Roy.

'Thanks,' said Alice.

Roy picked up Space Dog's lead. He was ready to leave. He hardly listened as Manya went on to the last award.

'The last rosette is for Cutest Dog in the show,' she said. 'And first place goes to Roy's adorable curly-haired canine— Space Dog!'

'Roy! You've won!' Alice screamed. 'You've won a prize!'

Roy was so surprised he could hardly move. In a daze, he led Space Dog up to Fred and Manya. Fred gave Roy the blue rosette. It said CUTEST DOG in gold letters.

'Congratulations, Roy,' said Fred. 'You have a very cute dog.'

'Thank you,' said Roy.

They all looked at Space Dog, who was hanging his head.

'Look!' said Manya. 'He's being modest.'

'I don't know,' said Roy. 'He might be feeling sick.'

Chapter 8

The Cutest Dog in Town

Space Dog felt miserable as he and Roy walked home from the park. 'Cutest dog!' he said. 'I'll never live this down.'

Roy was holding the rosette in his hand. He looked at it again and again. He didn't care what they had won it for. He was just happy to have a blue rosette—at long last.

'Being called cute isn't the worst of it,' Space Dog went on. 'The worst part is that Blanche, the most brainless creature I've ever seen—and that includes certain bloblike life forms on Mars—Blanche won the first place for Most Intelligent!'

'But we won a prize, didn't we?' said

Roy. 'That's what counts.'

'You don't even care, do you?' said Space Dog unhappily. 'You don't care that I, your friend, who got nothing but triple excellent marks in school, have just been insulted! I entered that pet show to uphold my dignity and what happened? They called me cute!'

'Of course I care,' said Roy. 'But really, what is so bad about being cute?'

'You Earth people are all alike,' said Space Dog. 'You have no respect for advanced brain power.'

With that, Space Dog stopped talking. They were home.

Roy ran inside the house. 'Mum! Dad!' he called. 'Look!'

Mr and Mrs Barnes were in the living room. 'What is it, Roy?' asked Mrs Barnes.

'We won!' said Roy. 'Space Dog won this blue rosette!' He showed it to his parents.

'It says Cutest Dog,' said Mrs Barnes. 'Oh Roy, it's wonderful!' She gave her son a hug.

'Good job, Roy,' said Mr Barnes. 'You, too, doggie. Well done.' He patted Space Dog on the head. Then he shook Roy's hand. 'Let's go upstairs and hang that rosette on the wall in your room.'

Everyone went up to Roy's room. Mr Barnes hung the rosette up. 'There,' he said. 'It looks terrific. And there's lots of space left for all the other prizes you'll win some day.'

'Thanks, Dad,' said Roy. He was beaming with pride. The rosette did look nice on the wall.

When Mr and Mrs Barnes went back downstairs, Space Dog said, 'Your parents certainly were excited.'

'Of course,' said Roy. 'It's good to win things. You should be happy.'

'I *am* happy,' said Space Dog. 'I'm happy for you. I'm glad you have a rosette. You deserve it.'

'No, Space Dog,' said Roy. '*You* deserve it. You were really nice to enter the pet show at all. I know you didn't want to. Only a real friend would have done it.'

'Go on,' said Space Dog. 'It was nothing.'

'And, anyway,' said Roy, as he put his arm around his friend, '*I* know how intelligent you are. And *you* know how intelligent you are. Who cares what anyone else thinks?'

Space Dog smiled. 'You're right,' he said.

Roy smiled back. 'On the other hand, you *are* pretty cute,' he said.

Space Dog picked up a pillow. He held it up over his head and said, 'What did you call me?'

'Cutesy-wootsy!' said Roy, reaching for another pillow. 'Ouch!' he said as Space

Dog thumped him.

'Gotcha!' said Space Dog. 'I dare you to call me "cute" again!'

'Adora-worable!' said Roy, and he bashed Space Dog back.

'Cut it out!' said Space Dog, pretending to be serious. 'You're messing up my lovely curls!'

Bash!

In the end they were both laughing so hard they could hardly lift their arms.

What a day! Not only had they won a rosette, but the boy and his very unusual dog were better friends than ever.